AN EID STORY

HUSNA
AND THE
EID PARTY

Fawzia Gilani-Williams

Illustrated by Kulthum Burgess

MUSLIM CHILDREN'S LIBRARY
THE EID STORIES SERIES
Husna and the Eid Party
Author: Fawzia Gilani-Williams
Illustrator: Kulthum Burgess
Book Design: Stratford Design
Coordinator: Anwar Cara

Published by
The Islamic Foundation
Markfield Conference Centre
Ratby Lane, Markfield
Leicestershire, LE67 9SY
United Kingdom

T: (01530) 244 944 F: (01530) 244 946
E: publications@islamic-foundation.com

Quran House, PO Box 30611, Nairobi, Kenya

PMB 3193, Kano, Nigeria

British Library Cataloguing in Publication Data

Gilani-Williams, Fawzia
    Husna and the Eid party. - (An Eid story) (Muslim children's library)
    1. Ramadan - Juvenile fiction 2. Friendship - Juvenile fiction 3. Children's stories
    I. Title II. Burgess, Kulthum III. Islamic Foundation (Great Britain)
    823.9'2[J]

ISBN-13: 9780860374060

Printed by Proost International Book Production, Belgium

Husna had lots of friends at school. She liked
them all very much because they always did
activities together, but most of all she liked
Maryam because Maryam was so much fun.
One day, when Husna was in the school
playground, she heard Muslimah shout over to
Maryam, "Where's the party going to be?"
"I'm not sure," said Maryam, "probably at the
house."

Husna thought Maryam was having a late *Eid* Party. *Eid* had been last week. She couldn't wait to get home to see if she had received an invitation. Husna ran out of her classroom. But Sister Khadijah, her teacher, stopped her. "Come back, Husna, and try that again," she said.
Husna sighed. "Sorry, Sister Khadijah, I shouldn't be running in school," she apologised.

Then as she was leaving her locker, she swung around so quickly that she bumped into Sister Sarah, the Arabic teacher.
"*Subhanallah*, Husna," said Sister Sarah. "Be careful."
"Sorry, Sister Sarah, *ana asifa*, I'm so sorry," Husna apologised.

Husna ran from the school all the way home.
"Mum, *As-Salamu 'Alaikum!*" she said breathlessly. "Is there any mail for me?"
"*Wa 'Alaikum as-Salam!*" replied her mother. "I

haven't checked. Could you check the mailbox for me, please?"

"Oooh! Mum, of course I can!" replied Husna and without another word she rushed off to the mailbox. When she looked inside there were lots and lots of letters.

She carefully pulled them out. She hurried back into the house and placed them on the kitchen table. She looked through them one by one. She let out a deep groan when she looked at the last one. None of them were addressed to her.

"Subhanallah! Mum, none of these letters are for me," complained Husna.

"But that's not unusual, Husna darling," explained Mum. "You usually don't get mail."

Just then the phone began to ring.

"Oooooooooooh!" squealed Husna. *"Insha' Allah,* it's for me! It's Maryam! She wants to invite me to her party!"
Husna ran to the phone. "Can I answer it, Mum? Please?" begged Husna.
Mum thought for a moment, wondering who it might be and then nodded.

"As-Salamu 'Alaikum!" said Husna.
"Wa 'Alaikum as-Salam, Husna!" replied Maryam. "How are you?"

"Al-Hamdulillah! Oooh! It is you! I thought it would be you!" beamed Husna.

"I'm sorry to bother you, I hope I didn't interrupt your tea," continued Maryam, "but I forgot to write down the *hadith* that Sister Khadijah gave us in class today, and is Sister Sarah giving us a test on *Surah Tin* on Wednesday?"

"The test is on Friday," said Husna, "let me get the *hadith*." Husna hurried to her school bag and pulled out her homework planner. Husna slowly read the *hadith*. When she had finished Husna asked, "So, Maryam, are you doing anything interesting this weekend?"

"I don't think so. Nothing exciting anyway," said Maryam. *"Jazakillahu khairan* for the help, Husna. *Insha' Allah* I'll see you at school tomorrow," and she hung up the phone.

"Barak Allah fi-ki," sighed Husna, wondering why Maryam hadn't told her about the party.

"Well I don't have to be invited to every *Eid* party in the whole wide world!" Husna told herself.

Husna finished her homework and then helped her mum clear the table. But she couldn't keep her mind off the *Eid* party. She kept on wondering why Maryam hadn't invited her.

Soon it was time for *Salat-ul-Maghrib*.

"Mum," called Husna, "it's time to pray *Maghrib.*"

"Do you have *wudu?*" asked her mother.

"No, *Insha' Allah* I will make it now."

As Husna climbed the staircase to the bathroom, she chanted, "She will invite me, she won't invite me, she will invite me, she won't invite me," until she climbed to the top step. "She won't invite me!" Husna's face fell into a grimace.

She walked into the bathroom and then stopped suddenly, "Oh oh!" she exclaimed. She walked backwards out of the bathroom and then said her *du'a*.

"O Allah, I seek refuge with You from all evil and those who do evil," then she went into the bathroom. She brushed her teeth and then did her *niyyah* and made *wudu*.

Husna knew that *sujud* was the best time to make a special *du'a* to Allah.

"Allah is very close to the believers when they are in *sujud*, so make many beautiful *du'as* when you are in *sujud!*" her mother would always say. Husna prayed *Salat-ul-Maghrib* in *jama'at* with her mum. "Dear Allah, please help Maryam remember to invite me to her *Eid* party," prayed Husna.

Husna dreamed all night long about Maryam's *Eid* party. She dreamed about *somosas* and kebabs, *mithai* and *rasmalai*, about games and treasure hunts, balloons and pass the parcel. In the morning she got up feeling wonderful. After offering *Salat-ul-Fajr*, Husna hurriedly put on her school uniform and gobbled down her breakfast. She couldn't wait to go to school.

"I'll drop you off," said her dad. "I have a meeting so I have to leave at eight."
Husna was so thankful. "That means I'll get to school quite early!"

During school, Husna tried so many different ways to ask Maryam if she had forgotten to invite her to the party.

She tried to ask during the reading lesson but Sister Khadijah shouted out, "I hope you're reading and not talking little girl!"

In Arabic class Husna tried to send a note to Maryam but Sister Sarah thought it was for her, and picked it up and put it on her desk.

At lunch time Husna saw Maryam in the lunch line talking to Nabilah and Afia who were in grade two. She raced over to them. But a big girl in grade seven called Tahirah, shouted out, "Hey that's *haram!* You can't push in! I'm telling Sister Hala, the principal!"

Husna went back to her seat in the cafeteria and began eating her lunch but she could hardly take a mouthful. She was so miserable!

During recess Husna saw Maryam playing skipping with two girls in their class. Every time Husna tried to talk to her, Rahimah and Diana kept telling her to keep clear of the skipping rope as they turned it for Maryam.

In Computer Studies Husna typed a message to Maryam but Muzzammil, a boy in her class, accidentally deleted it.

During *Jumu'ah*, Husna sat right next to Maryam but Sister Zahirah, the Kindergarten teacher, had told all the children that no one was allowed to talk during the *khutbah* or they might lose their blessings from Allah and get a detention. Husna tried to concentrate on the *khutbah* but it was very hard. After *Salat-ul-Jumu'ah*, Maryam had to move to a different spot to offer her *sunnah* prayer

It was the end of the day when Husna finally saw Maryam. She was sitting in Brother Umar's bus. Brother Umar was the school bus driver and drove the children home after school. Husna waved to Maryam and ran towards the bus.
"Have a wonderful weekend!" she cried. "I hope you enjoy tomorrow!"

Maryam gave Husna a big smile and waved
frantically back to her.

Husna let out a deep sigh as she saw Maryam's
bus drive away. She felt so bad inside. "She didn't
invite me to her *Eid* party," sniffed Husna. Big
tears swelled in her eyes and a lump came in her
throat. She felt terrible.

Husna walked home with her head down and shoulders drooped.

When she got into the house her mum greeted her with a big happy smile. *'As-Salamu 'Alaikum,* Husna!" said Mum. "Did you have a nice day? Aren't you glad it's Friday?"

Husna put her arms around her mother and began to sob. Between her sobs she told her mother that Maryam had not invited her to her *Eid* party.

Mum tried to make Husna feel better. "Firstly, Husna," explained Mum, "I understand how you feel. We all like to be included in special events. When we are not, then we feel heartbroken. Secondly, Husna tell me, how many excuses did you make for Maryam? Allah asks us to make excuses for our brothers and sisters if they do something that upsets us. Thirdly, sometimes

we get disappointed because we can't have what we want, but we should ask Allah for patience, *sabr jamil*."

Husna felt better after Mum sat with her. Mum was always so good at giving examples of the Prophets of Allah and talking about their hardships and patience.

The next day was Saturday. Dad had to go to the store to buy supplies for his office and so he took Husna with him. On the way back they drove past Maryam's house. There were balloons everywhere. Husna looked away sadly, *"La ilaha illallah,* I'm not invited to the party," she told herself.

When she got home, the phone was ringing. Husna jumped up wondering whether Maryam had finally remembered to ask her to come to the party.

Husna quickly asked for permission to answer the phone. Dad was busy making Mum some tea, so he nodded to Husna.

"As-Salamu 'Alaikum, peace be with you," said Husna excitedly. The voice at the other end was Hajrah's mum, Sister Hafsa.

Hajrah was in Grade one and Husna was her reading pal.

"How are you, Husna?" asked Hajrah's mum.
"*Al-Hamdulillah,* I'm fine," answered Husna.
"Thank you for being Hajrah's reading pal. She loves the books you read to her in school."
"Thank you, I enjoy reading to Hajrah too," replied Husna.
After a while Husna called to her mum. "Hajrah's mum wants to talk with you, Mum!"

Mum spoke with Hajrah's mum. A little later she looked across at Husna with a smile and said, "Get ready Husna! We're going to the mosque to meet some friends; they're having pizza and games after prayer!"

Husna jumped up and down, she was so happy.

When Husna arrived at the mosque car park she saw Maryam coming out of Sister Hafsa's car.

"Maryam! Maryam!" cried Husna. "What are you doing here? Why aren't you at your party?"

Maryam ran over to Husna. "Oh, the party was for my brother, Muhammad and his friends! Sister Hafsa dropped off her son, Munim, so he could be at the party and then she brought me here to play with you and some other friends!"

"*Subhanallah*, Maryam, I was so miserable, I thought you had forgotten to invite me!" said Husna.

"I could never do that, Husna, I could never forget you!" laughed Maryam.

Husna let out a big sigh and gave Maryam a big hug.

"Come on!" said Husna cheerfully. "Let's play!"

GLOSSARY

Al-Hamdulillah – Praise be to God.

ana asifa – I am sorry.

As-Salamu 'Alaikum – Peace be with you.

Barak Allah fi-ki – The blessing of God be with you.

Du'a – Supplication, prayer.

Eid-ul-Fitr – The first major Islamic festival celebrated to mark the end of Ramadan.

Eid-ul-Adha – The second major Islamic festival celebrated towards the end of Hajj.

hadith – Saying of the Prophet Muhammad ﷺ.

haram – Forbidden.

Insha' Allah – God willing.

jama'at – Congregation.

Jazakillahu khairan – May God give you best of rewards.

Friday khutbah – Sermon given before Friday congregational prayer.

La ilaha illallah – There is nothing worthy of worship except God.

mithai – Indian sweets.

niyyah – Intention.

rasmalai – Indian sweet dish.

sabr jamil – Beautiful patience.

Salat-ul-Fajr – A prescribed act of worship offered before dawn.

Salat-ul-Jumu'ah – Friday congregational worship.

Salat-ul-Maghrib – A prescribed act of worship offered at sunset.

samosa – A fried pastry filled with vegetables and/or meat.

Subhanallah – Glory be to God.

sujud – Prostrating on the ground to God.

sunnah – Acts done by the Prophet Mohammad ﷺ.

Surah Tin – 95th chapter in the Qur'an.

Wa 'Alaikum as-Salam – And peace be on you.

Wudu – Ablution: a system of washing prior to prayer.